SCRUMPY

For Katie, Caroline and Jenny, who loved Scrumpy.
And Scrumpy, who loved them — E.D.

Text copyright ©1994 by Elizabeth Dale. Illustrations copyright ©1994 by Frédéric Joos.
This paperback edition first published in 2001 by Andersen Press Ltd.
The rights of Elizabeth Dale and Frédéric Joos to be identified as the author and illustrator of
this work have been asserted by them in accordance with the Copyright, Designs and Patents
Act, 1988. First published in Great Britain in 1994 by Andersen Press Ltd., 20 Vauxhall Bridge
Road, London SW1V 2SA. Published in Australia by Random House Australia Pty., 20 Alfred
Street, Milsons Point, Sydney, NSW 2061.All rights reserved. Colour separated in Switzerland
by Photolitho AG, Zurich.Printed and bound in China.

10 9 8 7 6 5 4 3 2 1

British Library Cataloguing in Publication Data available.

ISBN 0 86264 703 7

This book has been printed on acid-free paper

SCRUMPY

Written by Elizabeth Dale
Illustrated by Frédéric Joos

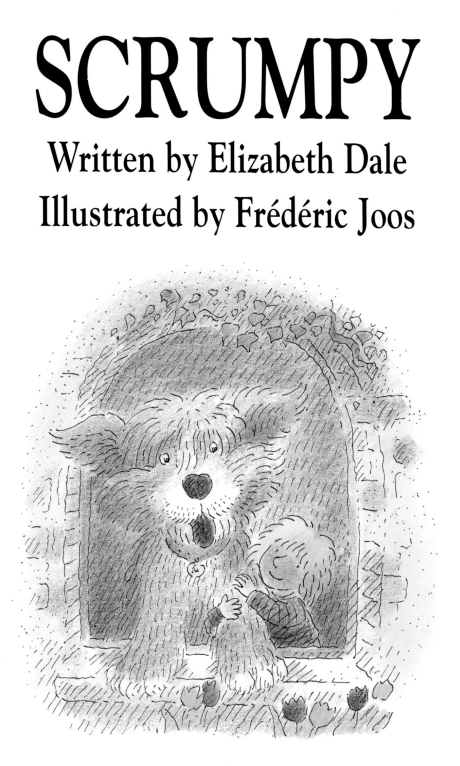

Andersen Press • London

Ben had a dog called Scrumpy.

He was more than a dog, he was a very special friend.

They went everywhere
together. To the park...

to the beach...

to the shops.

Ben loved nothing more than taking
Scrumpy for a walk ... or rather being
taken for a walk by Scrumpy!

When Ben returned home from school,
Scrumpy was always the first to greet him,
with bright eyes and a big red tongue!

One day, Scrumpy wasn't there to greet
Ben when he came home.
"He isn't very well," said Ben's mum.
"I expect he'll be better in the morning."

But Scrumpy was worse. Ben's father took him
to the vet, who gave Scrumpy some pills,

and Ben's mum allowed Scrumpy to sleep
in Ben's bedroom each night.

Two days later, Scrumpy
died. Ben couldn't bear it.
He didn't want Scrumpy
to die. How could he
live without him?

Ben's mum held him tight and told him it
was good to cry. She said that Scrumpy had
had a very bad pain, but now he was free
from that, so they should be glad.

But Ben couldn't be glad. He felt he had Scrumpy's pain. He couldn't sleep and all he could think about was Scrumpy. He missed him so much.

Ben's family buried Scrumpy in the garden, beneath the apple tree. Afterwards they all went inside to have tea, but Ben just sat by the window staring out.

When he went to the park,
Ben saw a dog chasing after
a stick.

When he went to the shop,
Ben saw another boy buying
a tin of dog food.

When he went to the beach,
Ben saw a dog jumping into
the waves. Every time he
remembered Scrumpy it hurt.

Ben stopped going to the park or the shop
or the beach. Instead he played football with
his friends.

Ben's mum didn't like to see him looking so
unhappy. "Would you like to get another dog?"
she asked him.
"No!" cried Ben. "Never! There'll never be
another Scrumpy." And he ran upstairs and
flung himself on his bed, and cried and cried
and cried.

Weeks passed and each day
Ben tried not to think of Scrumpy.
Then one fine spring morning, when Ben was
playing football in the street, he nearly tripped over a cat
racing down the pavement, followed by a large brown dog,
chased by a very cross man.
"Miaowwww!" cried the cat.
"Wuff, wuff, WUFF!" barked the dog.
"GEORGIE, STOP!!" shouted his owner.

"Ahh!" cried a man, as the cat ran under his ladder.
CLATTER, BANG! went the paint tin. HONK! went
the car horn, SCREECH! went the lorry's brakes.

OH, GEORGIE!

The cat disappeared through a tiny hole in a fence. Georgie ran back to his owner and leapt up at him, licking him cheerfully.

"Oh, Georgie!" cried the man. Ben laughed. He couldn't help it. He laughed and laughed so much, he thought he'd never stop. He laughed at the dog, at the man, but most of all because he remembered a time when Scrumpy had knocked over a paint tin when his dad was painting the gate.

As Ben walked up to the back door, he could
still see the green foot-prints on the path. He
sat on the step and recalled the fun he'd had
with Scrumpy, and suddenly, for the first time,
he was glad for all the times they'd shared and
that Scrumpy had been his friend.

"Can we have another
dog, after all?" he asked
his mum.
"Of course!" said his
mum and hugged him.

It was difficult choosing a new dog. There were so many adorable puppies to pick from.

But then, as soon as he saw her, Ben knew which one they should have.

Ben called his new puppy Honey.

She didn't look like Scrumpy. She wasn't a bit
like Scrumpy. She would never, ever, take
Scrumpy's place...

... but she was still a special friend to Ben.

A

Andersen Press paperback picture books